Un Lugar Lejos

Un Lugar Lejos

VALLEYS

GREGG YUPANKI BAUTISTA

Echo Thread Books

Published by Echo Thread Books, an imprint of Echo Thread Projects, in the United States of America.

www.echothreadprojects.com

This collection is a work of fiction. Characters, incidents, and dialogue are drawn from the author's imagination. Any resemblance to actual events or persons, living or dead, is entirely coincidental.

Designed and illustrated by Gregg Yupanki Bautista
www.greggbautista.com

Typeset in EB Garamond

ISBN: 979-8-218-43150-1

*To my abuelita, who birthed my indigenous pride
in a shower of iridescent fish scales, and taught me to
never be ashamed of where my history comes from.*

*To my father, who I remember would listen to the huaynos from a
home he missed when I was young, staying true to who he was while
learning to understand a new world.*

*To those who ever felt lost or othered because of what
they look or sound like, or where they are from.*

Adelante con corazón.

CONTENTS:

A ENTENDER (Español)

Ojos distantes
observan flores celestiales
mientras que oscurecen
y las memorias se retiran

Una pluma cae
recibido por la brisa
que acaricia las nubes
y los guía a través de las cumbres

Pero la pluma permanece
      arremolinándose
         cayéndose
mientras él estira su mano

Es en ese momento
que se da cuenta
que entiende
que se despertara en un lugar nuevo
un lugar lejos

UNDERSTANDING (English)

Distant eyes
watch celestial flowers
as they darken
and memories fade

A falling feather
is taken up by the breeze
that caresses the clouds
and leads them across the summits

But the feather remains
     swirling
          falling
while he reaches for it

It's in that moment
that he realizes
that he understands
that he would wake up in a new place
a faraway place

ECHOES IN THE VALLEY

The old voice calls me back,
and I feel the earth sing beneath my feet.
Her skin is warm soil, a generous promise of life.
Old friend
Old mother
Pachamama.
I feel us moving together
in time
through time
our momentum
in rhythm.

I think of this as I watch the sky, listening
to the sound of the stars
washing over me and the sleeping mountain.
What wonders have the stars seen?
How far have they traveled?
What stories do they know?
My own stories have become untethered from me,
displaced me,
therefore losing me.

I've dived deep into the sky river Mayu,
swam with the yana phuyu,
the dark clouds of the galaxy.

Was it with them that I left something behind?
Was it there
that I entrusted some time
while floating through the space matter of histories
long disintegrated,
among the potentials
of worlds-to-be?
A telling rumble crawls between the stars -

I've seen this before,
a dream has shown me this moment.
That's how I made it here, knowing
when the eyes must be readied.

These recurrences are quick.

Sky river Mayu opens across the heavens,
pouring out from an invisible tearing seam.
It pulses,
its depth flows and undulates into itself,

waves rippling out into golden halos.
From within,
slowly,
with the gentleness that the expanse
of infinity affords them,
the yana phuyu wake,
and gold
and ruby
and sapphire eyes open.

How beautiful, those colossal beings.
They are darker than the night,
and you'll find them on the darkest ones,
visible only if you stop,
welcome,
and watch the sky for their eyes to find you.
Eyes that sparkle in the cosmos,
often hidden
by our fear of slowing down,
of accepting the dark as a truth
and not a symptom
of regress.

Then

Whispers
from the sky,
quiet calls.
Their echoes grow
louder,
cascading
down
the valley walls.
If we open our minds,
we can be in the now and then.

We'll listen
as they tell us
that we will follow time into the sun.

What chance is there to make sense of this?
I've searched
for as long as I can remember.

But the search is all
I remember.

THE AFTER

Every once in a while, a persistent ringing fills my ears, boring into my mind and excavating a place to plant itself.

One such time, I was walking a mountain trail near Calca in search of a huaca. I heard that the monument stood watch over an old fortress of red stone and adobe. Walking through the valley with the river to my right, I changed course to a nearby hilltop in hopes of checking my bearings from the higher vantage point. With no luck at first, only seeing desert on one side of the hills and the valley on the other, I made my way from hilltop to hilltop while keeping the river below to my right.

Half way down one particular hill, I passed between a pair of stone towers mostly covered in grass and moss, and I would have missed the little village down the slope if the sun were at any angle other than its mid-day peak.

The green tree foliage swayed in the breeze and its color contrasted against the reddish clay structures, revealing the deteriorating thatched roofs that otherwise blended in with the soft yellows of the hillside's winter grass.

A dirt path further down the hill looked like a nice break from the rocky terrain, so I made my way through the spread of tall growth with its clusters of bromeliads of all shapes and sizes bordering the village.

As I drew nearer, I noticed the grounds of the hill faces were divided into agricultural terraces, barren except for the same winter grasses I saw on my way in. The entrance to the village was scattered with stone foundations, either unfinished or long collapsed.

I approached one structure that seemed the most intact, perhaps a home, with walls of stones and crumbling clay bricks. I felt an urge to knock but the door didn't look very sturdy.

A little square opening past the doorway caught my eye. I looked in, unsure what I would find. The space inside was empty, save for a short wooden bench in the far corner with withered grasses strewn about the floor. I did find it peculiar that the gray thatched roof had patches of freshly dried winter grass woven in. Surveying the other remnants, there were no indications of someone being present that would make such repairs. The only sounds around me were my footsteps and the breeze brushing past me, rustling the leaves throughout the hillside.

A distant staccatoed braying broke the quiet. I couldn't tell how far it was, but then it came again from farther in the village. Curious, I followed it in hopes of coming across the animal, perhaps even a herder. It's been a few days since I've encountered someone in the valley, let alone had clear direction to the fortress.

Continuing across a clearing and following the occasional bray, I came to a set of stone steps that led down to another terrace level. A llama looked up at me from the grass. No braying came now that we were face to face.

That's where I met the old man.

He sat on a low, mossy rock wall under the shade of a small wooden hut. A pair of wooden walking staves rested across his lap. A fading multicolored woven chullo rested over his graying hair, and a stringy white beard poked out from under his chin and rested on the oversized knot of his manta shawl. I noted the beard because his llama, eying me as if I had no business showing up unannounced, had a similar scraggly beard that waggled in the air as it chewed the grass.

Looking me over from his seat on the wall with less skepticism about my appearance than the llama, the old man asked if I was lost. Anyone could surmise I was not exactly equipped to be wandering the hills and mountains, so his question seemed more like an observation. I had no possessions other than my travel-worn mask and the clothes I wore, still laced with the dust from the roads of Yuncaypata.

His "¿Estás perdido?" - *Are you lost?* - felt more like a *"You're lost, aren't you?"*

I saw no point in denying it, sensing no unkindness behind the question.

He nodded in return and turned back towards his llama, who had lost interest in me and wandered off to a new patch of grass. But the old man's attention was directed at a tuft of white hair flanked by a pair of fuzzy gray ears sticking out from the grass where the llama had been standing. Two little black eyes looked from the old man, to me, and back.

"¡Ven!" called the old man, motioning for me to come down the stairs and share the spot on the wall next to him. The llama's cria, the owner of the little tuft of hair, crouched into the safety of the grass and watched me approach. The old man reached up under his beard, unknotting his manta to reveal a satchel. Before I could ask anything about where I was or if he knew anything about the fortress, he opened his pack and asked if I was hungry. I said I was alright, but a growl from my empty stomach betrayed my attempt to decline taking his food.

From his satchel, the old man produced fist-sized loaves of bread, avocados, cooked potatoes wrapped in leaves, hard boiled eggs, and a pair of fruits I had only seen once before - granadilla. He divided the meal in half on the wall between us and pulled a canteen from the pack, which he held out and shook at me. A tight slosh came from inside to prove its fullness, making me wonder how long he had actually been sitting out here, questioning if this perfectly rationed meal was chance or providence.

He asked my name as I drank, and I took a moment before responding - I was still having trouble remembering much of anything, and it had been almost two weeks and many miles since I found myself standing on Pachatusan mountain, as the locals called it. So I gave him the name I remembered best at that moment.

"Yupanki," he repeated. "Muy bien," either approving of the introduction or the name.

He took back the canteen, pocketed the top, and stood with the help of his staves. I observed how he hunched as he made his way over to the baby llama, but also noticed how his shuffles were deliberate and sure footed. Graceful, even. He emptied some water into his hand and held it out for the cria to drink. Once the cria was content, he capped the canteen and shuffled back over, sat with a groan, and turned to me with a smile.

"Where did you come from?" he asked.

I began explaining my trek through Yuncaypata, but he shook his head and asked again, emphasizing the "where" and "from." I realized I misunderstood his question as he motioned towards the state of my clothes. I said I didn't know, told him about the mountain I found myself on, and what I was looking for despite not knowing where I was headed. I told him it had been a few weeks, that progress and remembering were slow.

A few minutes passed as we ate in silence, and he asked if I had found my time yet. The question didn't make sense, so I asked what he meant.

"Tú sabes, viajero," he said while he peeled an egg, "la puerta a tu tiempo." *You know, traveler, the door to your time.* He bit the egg in half, and between chews said, "¿Sabes que? Deja que te ayude."

"*A door to my -*" I began to ask, still not understanding, but he started flickering in and out of being as we sat there. The ringing began, loud, and his words hung in the air as the world around me shimmered and changed.

"Viajero," he called me. *Traveler.*

The ringing quieted to a gentle pulse as the world continued wavering in and out of clarity through iridescent ripples. Everything doubled and tripled, continuing to multiply and simultaneously fold into itself, the way a dahlia's blooming petals fold into the nexus of its center.

The empty village began to fill with life.

Green grasses, paths well kept, foundations that were in shambles a moment ago were now completed structures of homes and granaries. The land terraces flowed with greens and golds and purples of summer in their abundance of maize and quinoa. Children ran about playing, while some adults fed leaf wrapped vegetables and meats into a pit and covered them with hot stones. The people wore garments similar to the old man, some with brightly colored belts, skirts, or vests. Weavers sang unfamiliar words at their looms, their voices carrying in the warm breeze. Rhythmic CLACKS accented the songs as another distant group laid the foundations for a wall that would become a new terrace. A hungry baby cried. Men and women called to each other across fields, but like the songs, I didn't understand the words.

As everything around me coalesced into a single world, the old man sitting before me now sat a little straighter. He seemed younger, clothes the same but more vibrant, his complexion a little ruddier and features a bit smoother. His hair had darkened, and his eyes retained the same kindness earned by the long life of an old man who could offer a stranger a meal without a second thought.

His voice, stronger now, greeted me in the language being spoken and sung all around me, echoing thousands of years of history. When he spoke, his words plucked at threads in the furthest depths of my memory.

"Alli p'unlla." *Good morning.*

Morning again? Wasn't it just the afternoon?

"I'm happy you're finally here," he continued, *"I've been waiting for quite some time, viajero."*

"Where am I?" I asked, surprised at the ease this old language came to me.

"Still where we were a moment ago," he said, *"but in a different 'when.' I brought you through to my time because it's easier to be here, at least for me. This 'when' is long, long ago to yours."*

I couldn't shake the feeling of having been in this new place before, but found it hard to believe that I was actually there. I had never Shifted like we did just then, without a mask, yet it happened so seamlessly and naturally.

The herder, no longer appearing frail, gathered his manta pack and staves, waving towards a road that cut through the center of the main section of the village, and I followed.

"Is it any easier for you here?" he asked. *"Can you remember?"*

"Remember what?" I responded.

A dog barked and ran across the road in front of us, chasing after a small animal that darted across just out of its reach.

"Anything," he shrugged. *"Who you are. Where you're from."*

"No," I said shaking my head. *"Nothing. Just 'Yupanki.'"*

We went on, stopping occasionally for the man to chat with a villager in the old language, or for us to help with small tasks here and there - setting foundation stones into place, stirring boiling dye pots, fixing a plow.

After a loop around the village and some more questions to try to surface any memories, we ended up back at the terrace wall where we first met.

"Why did you bring me here? To this time?" I finally asked.

"Your time is not an easy one," he sighed. *"It's very confusing, and it's collected too much of itself to maintain clarity."* He waved a staff towards the village and continued, *"When I first came here, there wasn't much. Small groups of people scattered throughout the hills, living simply on what the land offered. Together, we built this into a place that could support itself and mutually benefit from others nearby and in other parts of the valley. I watched over everyone in exchange for their commitment to each other and ensured no harm would come to them."*

I asked what happened to all the people, and why the village was empty in my time.

"Well," he replied, *"in time, as is the nature of things, we were forgotten as empires around us came and went."*

There were more questions coming to mind than answers I was getting, but we were starting to wander from my original question.

"What does any of that have to do with bringing me here?" I asked.

"Oh yes," he said. *"The 'why' and the 'when.' That kind of time, in this instance, doesn't mean anything. I am hoping that some*

time in this when will clear something up for you. I only have so many answers."

We continued up the stairs, walking back towards where I first entered the village, eventually stopping at a stone path I hadn't noticed before. It was flanked by two knee-high stones carved with condor motifs. The space began to shimmer and my view was superimposed by a recollection of the village as I first saw it - vacant and overgrown. The vision dissolved as quickly as it came and the path was visible again. Atop each condor missing from my "when" grew a blooming bromeliad, the flowers protruding from protective leafy blades. These flower-topped statues appeared to guard a path that led down the side of the hill. Beyond where it dropped out of sight, I could see a short wooden bridge over a streamlet that divided the terraces towards the next hill.

I pointed, asking, *"Where does this go?"*

"Huchuy Qosqo," he said. *"Your red fortress. That might be a good place to search for answers. Unfortunately, it may also be forgotten when you arrive, so you'll have to contend with its keeper. It's best to approach carefully."*

I mentally sifted through what I could remember of our conversation - had I actually mentioned the red fortress?

We continued toward the structure I thought was somewhat still intact when I arrived at the village, the one with the small wood bench inside. But now, as the late afternoon sunlight hit the home's thatched roof, it shone like gold. The house seemed to come alive as the sun filtered through the leaves in the breeze and shadows danced across the adobe walls. It was as if the house was breathing. His llamas were resting in front of the house, the mother humming and nursing her little cria.

"We all have a home," he said, *"and this one is mine."* A soft bleat from the llama made the herder smile. *"And of course my two friends here."*

The herder leaned over to gently pet the llamas and they hummed in response. He invited me to do the same. Their fleece felt coarse between my fingers, and the little one nuzzled into my palm. As they looked up at us, the eyes of the mother and cria glistened like sapphires.

I've seen eyes like those before.

I was wandering in a memory of sky river Mayu when the herder stood back up. This time, he needed to lean onto his staves to straighten himself. He ambled to his door, and with a gentle tap from the top of one staff, the edges of the door shimmered with bright light. The door slowly opened before him and the aroma of sunlit earth came spilling out from within, along with light as golden as the illuminated roof.

"I'm sorry," I said as he entered the doorway, *"I didn't thank you for the meal and your help. I haven't even asked your name."*

"What is mine is for all to share. And here," he said, *"they called me Willaq Cocha."*

I was curious why he used "called" since this was supposed to be his "when," but before I could think to ask, the sound of gently tearing fabric swelled above me again. I became aware of the pulsing ring, which had actually been continuous since we arrived, but barely audible. The sun rapidly phased between setting and mid-day. It gradually settled high in the sky and the world quieted back down to a cool breeze, all that was left was a faint iridescent ripple resembling a tiny bird. A thought flashed in my mind:

"The wings of Colibri echo within me and open the gates to the After."

"Oye primo, estás bien?" said an old voice.

I looked back down, and the village was empty again. Still beautiful, but everything seemed a little... faded. The old herder chewed the last bit of his fruit as he hunched over his staves, appearing to have been watching me stare up at the sky as I stood before the empty home with the gray roof. The door was open and the interior was dark again, just the lonely bench in the corner.

I said I was fine, or at least that I thought I was fine and that I must have just lost myself for a moment, and closed the door. He looked at me deeply with eyes that spanned generations.

"De dónde dijiste que eres?" he asked. *Where did you say you were from?*

"No sé," I said and shook my head. I still wasn't sure.

"Mm," he replied, "eres viajero, y no tienes patria." *You're a traveler, and you have no homeland.*

I thought about that for a moment, then asked if he knew about Huchuy Qosqo.

A smile crept across his lips. "Quizás," he said, "quizás no estás tan perdido como crees, viajero." *Perhaps you aren't as lost as you think, traveler.*

"You keep calling me "viajero" like you mean something else by it," I said. *"Why?"*

He told me about people he heard of who can go through doors that others cannot see or understand - doors that lead to places and times that don't always belong to the ones who enter.

"You think I'm one of those people?" I asked.

"¿Que tu crees?" he shot back. *What do you think?*

"And what are these places?"

With one stick, he began drawing a spiral in the earth in front of him. After a few orbits , he drew a line straight through the spiral's center. *"They say there are spaces within places where things many eyes can't perceive exist,"* and he pointed at the gaps between the tail of the spiral where the straight line intersected them. *"Some argue they* can't *exist because you can't see them,"* he continued, *"and others think they can only be felt and seen with a clear mind."* He tapped his forehead with that last statement.

"So people can find these places through something like meditation?" I asked.

"Más o menos," he responded while he tipped a knobby open hand back and forth. *"A person can find them with practiced honing of their minds - they can catch glimpses of and commune with these other places, but not truly cross into them. But there are myths of special tools passed down through history that allow their users to make these kinds of doorways. Others allow the very world to be shaped. Some call these users prophets or seers these days, others call them aberrations. But those words dilute what they truly are."*

"Which is?" I pressed.

"Well, like I said, these are only myths, but apparently they can see between and move through other spaces and times that presently are or have already come and gone. Perhaps even the future, if you choose to view time as a cycle." He pointed at the spiral in the earth at our feet again, but this time traced the tip of his staff back and forth along the line intersecting the spiral. He shifted his weight and leaned towards me with a questioning look in his eyes.

"Creo que algo te esta buscando desde allí -" he started.

"No soy profeta," I interrupted.

Ignoring me and narrowing his eyes, he repeated, *"I think something is searching for you from there. Because with those marks on your hand..."* Pausing to lift the sleeve of my tunic with one of his staves to expose a tattooed arm filled with glyphs and symbols, he said, *"perhaps YOU are a time migrant."*

Then, laughing as though we were both in on some unspoken joke, he turned back up the road, calling "¡Ven!" over his shoulder for me to follow.

A time migrant? I thought to myself as he stopped before the spread of grass and bromeliads that covered the rest of the hill before it dropped out of sight to a lower terrace. He was poking around inside the tall grass with a walking staff.

Wait, I thought, *is this the same pathway?*

"Aqui," he said, and the staff's end hit not earth, but stone. I bent over and pushed aside a few clumps of the tall grass, and there they were - stones of eroded condor motifs topped with remnants of vegetation.

The herder's llamas brayed from down on terrace where we left them.

"Suerte," he said with a smile when I stood up, "espero que encuentres algo útil." *Good luck, I hope you find something helpful.* He began his shuffle back towards the stone steps.

"Disculpa, no te agradecí," started to come out of my mouth and I heard a distant doubling of myself telling the herder I didn't thank him. I asked for his name.

He slowed his pace down the stairs. *"Oh, well,"* he said, *"the priests named me 'William.' The name ended up suiting everyone, so it stayed with me."*

"Priests? So there are *still other people here?"* I asked.

"No, no," he said, *"this was also long ago"* and waved his hand to emphasize.

The old herder looked out across the valley for a moment, looking like he was remembering that long ago time. But I was trying to think faster. "William" sounded like "Willaq" and wasn't far from... A thought was beginning to surface.

"Bueno, Yupanki," he said, with a tap from a walking staff against the stones. "Adelante con corazón," and continued down the steps, disappearing from view.

Right then, I grasped the question that seemed obvious to ask - *What if his last name is also "Cocha?"*

"¡Espera!" I called and ran after William to catch him before he got too far. But when I got to the bottom steps, "William" was gone from that lower terrace. No old herder. No llama. No cria. The hillsides were vacant once again.

There was, however, the canteen of water left behind on the wall where we sat and shared a meal. I felt its replenished weight as I picked it up, expecting it to be nearly empty. Something told me it was there on purpose, and that its purpose was to continue on with me. I made a mental note that once this was over, perhaps I would come back and return the canteen.

I stood there for another moment, looking out across the valley. Reaching down to my belt, I ran my fingers along the frayed material of my mask. The familiar fibers centered me, and the weight of the remaining pendants comforted me. My mask has been the one constant along this journey. I closed my eyes and listened to the breeze. The scent of the valley was in the air. My skin felt the sun. I took a deep breath and opened my eyes. The sun had started its descent for the day, and just as the sun was sure of its daily journey, I knew I needed to continue my own.

I slung the canteen strap over my shoulder and made my way back up to the tall grass across the road. Taking my first step onto the stone path through all its overgrowth, I smelled the faint homely aroma of that warm earth from Willaq's home. I felt time quiver and thought:

"The wings of Colibri echo within me and open the gates to the After."

SOMOS VASOS

We are vessels born from sacred earths,
carried by a great vessel floating in the sea of eternity.
We are vessels of space and time,
dancing helixes of threads.

Mother Earth,
moments ago a mountain range,
stands before me.
The Matriarch.
Demon dogs heel behind her,
licking their wounds.
The Puma at her side
sways to the music of her voice.

If you pause for a moment,
you begin to feel
the essence of what creates the resonance within you,
defining the shape you take.
For we are often entwined in the life fabric
and can never imagine how it feels
to be the spinning spindle,

collecting what unwinds
from our lives,
and love,
and violence.

Pachamama,
whom I watched birth mountains and command legions
of stone warriors awoken from their earthly chasms,
spits into the ground at her feet and mixes
with delicate finger tips.
A gentle, caressing spiral into the wet earth.
I was reminded of tales of a man creating man
from breath and dirt.
But did he ever feel the tender touch
a mother's love could give?

She sculpts the air and lifts her hand.
A *keru,*
a vessel,
full of earth,
rises from the ground.
She presents it to me, whispering
about its age,
how it's not as old as the ones that were never made,

the ones that will not taste air,
but old nonetheless.

She sang a song of Los Olleros,
the ancient potters who shaped it when
First Mountain touched the sky.

The earth within,
reddish brown like her,
reddish brown like me.
The grains are the remnants
and echoes
of our destinies.
The color, she says,
is gift from the sun
worth more than a crown.
Her fingertips pinch from the contents
of what was once earth
but liquefies into blood at her touch.
A transmuted droplet rolls off her finger,
falling back into the keru
as earth.

What does it matter, she poses,
which vehicle history takes -
earth or blood, is it not the same?
Every grain and cell
full of light and potential that we all carry,
almost as old as time.
The light that makes us Children of the Sun
and guides us through our journeys
and back to the earth in the end.
For what we carry is the very marrow of the world.
How it's used will shape the next.
And as long as we carry this light
our blood will never run dry.

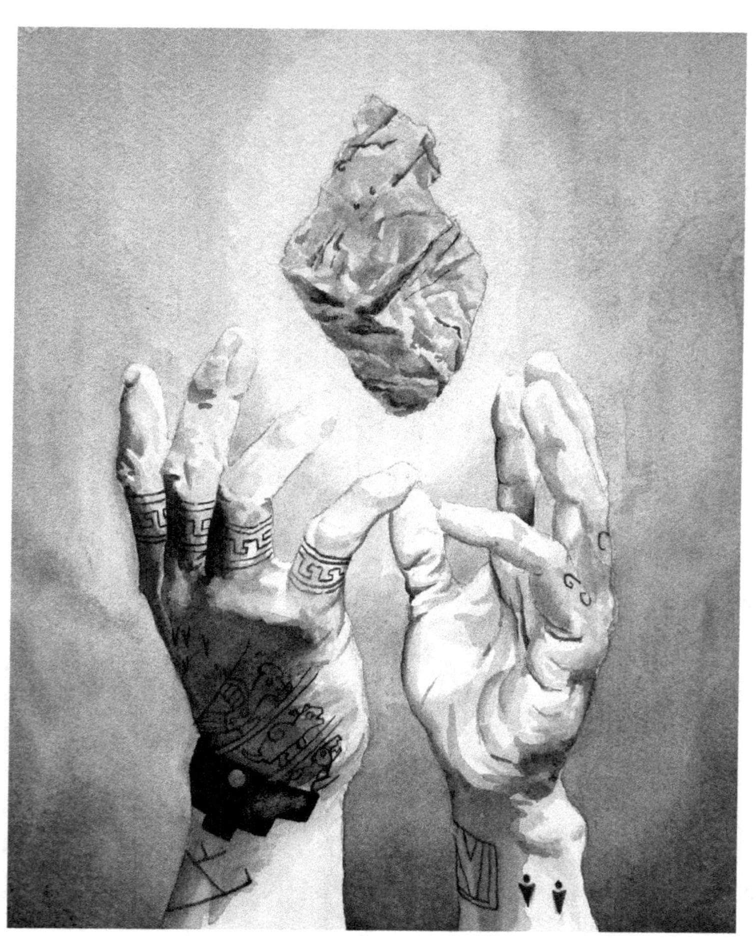

NOSTALGIA POR LO DESCONOCIDO

I have never been here
but it feels like it could be home.
I never left those lands
but I knew all the old roads here.

No gods,
your god
or my gods,
can deny

I will be born here,
as I have died there.

My skin, all marked and mapped,
serving as passage,
is welcomed to the posts
of spirits gone.
I carry a fragment
of this view in resonant stone
hidden within my mind,
guarded, safe, where no one can find.

It can take me across
the invisible canyons they made
in our homes, and I'm told
we'll be free if we can self-mend.

I can be anywhere
while standing here.
I can bring worlds to me,
unearth their roots,

Encounter other
lives that have been lived,
Places
and times
I've always
felt were mine.

Deep within, it's clear that
old ideas they thought kept me safe
were, in fact, my captors.
I can breathe, at last, and find home.

Because I knew the old roads here.

COLIBRI

A fire for a farewell
Embers jump and ride the updrafts
In an attempt to become stars

The crackles are the heartbeats
Of the ember hidden secrets
Spilling out for us to hear
For the night sky and me
There's an urgent hope in those sparks
Because perhaps
Given the proper circumstances
Could a spark not consume the world?

It could bring down empires
Make beggars of kings
And make way for the chance
Of a new world to be birthed

The seeds of the new world
Anxious to germinate
Glow steadily

As what waits beyond the fire
Watches
As I don my mask
For a final flight
A single pendant remaining
After all these years

Floating is a gossamer shimmer
No larger than a hummingbird
Because it is a hummingbird
A patient, tiny aurora
Here and not here
Beating its wings of iridescent light
Its tiny eyes watch me
Sympathetic to my uncertainty
Knowing the inevitability of pain
Brought by this change

I've seen what Colibri can do
And the effortlessness with which it's done

It's shown me that my very cells
Are incongruous with this world
As the earth struggles to live

So will my fabric be respun
So that I may clearly see
The wrongs that were committed
And I will meet the agents of hope
That will rewrite the unwritten

And we'll sing the songs of the silenced
And we'll see the dreams that are hidden
And we'll mend the hearts that are broken
And we'll gather those who are lost

Together Colibri and I
Will tear apart this reality
Of which I still know so little
Yet I hold dear what I've gathered
Because although my world
Contains so much in so little
It's still
So brittle

The Little Messenger hovers, watching me turn
These thoughts
Waiting to deliver me to Supay's door

So instead I think of the growing grass
Leaning toward me as I lay

Is it reaching for me
To pull me down
To see the world from its perspective?
I feel the pebbles between each blade
Bleached by the Sun
Soothed by the Moon
Smoothed by the Winds

From the kiss of the fire's light
They pulse an orange red
Like tiring suns
But they don't know that
They're only pebbles
Unaware how they arrived
Perhaps by glacier or flood
Or kicked along by passing feet
And perhaps they have a story
To sing into my ear
From when the earth was young
And the mountains were high
And the waters were pure

When the world didn't suffer
The conquests of brothers Hubris and Greed

So I lay my head down
And learn not all songs are joyous
Some stones dream of being a world
And fostering life
Or traveling the universe
And shining as a comet
While others lay silent
Dreaming to be world-crushing meteors

My eyes travel upwards to the sky
And I see the stars falling
Down towards the fire
And they play with the embers
While Colibri dances with the lights
Colliding into supernovas

I'm going blind now
I think it's happening
I had no warning
I once asked if death would hurt
To be pulled apart before rebirth

And Colibri only beats its wings
Telling me it's something to get used to

Now the stars kaleidoscope around the sky
Falling into a vortex of the spiraling embers
It dawns on me that the stars are no longer falling
Instead, I'm being pulled apart
Stretched across the galaxy
The stars instead rush past me
And for a moment I see
The very place we all exist
And how beautifully small we are
Because we think we're titans
Working so hard to find our place
In this place
And I expand further into darkness
Our galaxy now a speck

How can so many thoughts occur at once?

My cells are now long deteriorated
Scattering through dark matter
Some perhaps in a black hole somewhere
Bringing a fragment of me

To singularity
And I think of my cheek
Back on the cool night grass
With the fire that could change the world
And the pebbles that dreamt of the cosmos

I open my mind's eye
Looking to the mother mountain
And her voice says
Let go of these thoughts
And
It happens

I
                    c   om
                            e
                                    un d
                                        o
                                                ne

EPILOGUE

A red star begins to fade on the horizon in preparation to cross into its decline.

No... my daydream breaks and I see it's just the flicker of the dying campfire across the next hill crest. I've been following and closing distance between the camp's occupant and me for the past week.

Hidden from the naked eye by huacas, a crescent of boulders in this case, the small cave at the base of a boulder gave me reprieve from the sun and my pursuers. I meant to stay only while the sun was highest, but I must have drifted off if I was imagining dying stars. Fortunately, I still have a line of sight to keep watch of the whereabouts of who I've been trailing. Nervous that I'm too late, I get to my feet and try to climb down the cave entrance while attempting to ignore the onset of pins and needles creeping into my legs. The half moon overhead illuminates the landscape as I clumsily make my way through the sparse brush surrounding the huacas. A newborn fawn comes to mind as I half-hobble, half-sneak my way towards the camp, and I feel a little exposed in the open. But I'm propelled by the anticipation of finally meeting the prophet I've been tasked to find. We hope the prophet has some insight to why everything is changing, why Shifting is becoming so difficult to control.

I stay focused on the low fire, but it suddenly flares up into a column that reaches the sky - a serpent of fire striking out at the moon. From a few hundred feet away, I can still see the silhouette of the prophet being engulfed by the flames.

No! I think as the fire column begins to spin and waver around the prophet. My first thought is to run toward the fire, but I crouch low to the ground instead. I've come too far to be too reckless. I don't want to be the only thing moving around in this sudden surge of light. Anyone in this part of the desert will undoubtedly see this too. I'm impatient, but watch the fire whirl and recede back down to a weak burn. A long minute or two passes with no other surprises, so I continue onward, keeping quiet because now things don't feel right.

I finally get close enough to the camp to see the body laying on the freshly charred earth now surrounding the diminished campfire, and my breath catches in my throat because I already know what I'll find.

The figure is masked, its remaining fringes sizzle and crumble away and reveal part of a face underneath. I stand there and watch as more of the mask's threads smolder, revealing an eye, then a cheek. A nose. Lips. Dreams told me of the likeness, but I thought it was just an exaggeration brought on by the exhaustion of long days on foot. The face was my own, only older. Unsure what to do now, I move in and kneel for a closer look, thinking *this isn't the way it was supposed to happen.*

A rivulet of clean skin traces where a tear fell down the ashen cheek. A hand is clenched close to his chest, and something sticks out from his fist. I pull at the exposed threads and a small, ragged bundle of cloth comes out. Surprisingly, the exposed edges aren't burnt. I can feel a tiny object wrapped inside as I turn the little bundle in my hands and squeeze it between my fingers. Opening the cloth reveals a gold object the size of my pinky nail. White and orange from the moon and flames reflect off its cracked and hammered surface. I reach in and the moment my skin touches it, a voice echoes through my head:

"I'm sorry for not finding the path sooner. The keru is lost. Keep this pendant safe, and may the last of my mask help guide you with Colibri."

The last few words dissipate into the night, but I heard it all. No, "heard" isn't right. I *felt* it. But it doesn't matter, because I'm too late.

I comb my memory for anything I might remember from dreams about what just happened. I've seen the face, I've seen the pendant, but I don't remember the fire flaring. Nothing about a mask comes to mind, either. I have my own and have no business taking a second, especially one belonging to the prophet. What's left of his won't last much longer anyway, with the tiny embers hungrily devouring the frayed threads.

And who is Colibri? I think to myself.

I push away the idle thoughts and pull out the chuspa I carry with me, a gift from my grandmother - a little drawstring bag with hand-embroidered motifs from my favorite of her vases back home. I drop the pendant into the chuspa for safekeeping.

As if on cue, shouts ring out from across the hill, about a half mile back. Hunting dogs bark as flashlight beams cut through the night towards the camp. They've been on my trail ever since I started following after the now-dead prophet, but I thought I put more distance between us after I lost them at the river. The surge of fire is the only thing that would have led them to me so quickly.

"Shit," I mutter, chastising myself for my overconfidence and for not having put out the rest of the campfire when I arrived. I don't want to add "being found with a mysterious dead body" to my list of accolades with los tombos, they're as bad as la migra back home. But I've been found and need to improvise because these dogs are big and fast. I can hear their barks getting closer and closer. A truck engine revvs into sight, its floodlights breaching the hill crest. The flashlights are already closing in on their mark, guiding the truck's lights.

I clutch the chuspa close to my lips and close my eyes. I should have just enough time to make the trip before they reach an empty camp.

AFTERWORD

I intended for a version of this written collection of poems and short stories to come out alongside the music of *Un Lugar Lejos - EP* in August 2022. Back then, these were *very* short one- or two-liners. Not much of a "book," by any means.

I began performing the songs of *Un Lugar Lejos - EP* in late 2022, and they immediately began evolving from what I had just recorded and released at that point. Welcoming the changes to the music, I also embraced the changes that started occurring within the prose. The words morphed and multiplied, filling out the world of Yupanki more than I anticipated. The initial "glimpse" into his world quickly became the valley region he wandered for months, perhaps even years, over the course of these pages.

One of the most exciting and unexpected parts of continuing to write was that Yupanki met others along the way. We discovered William (or was it Willaq?) waiting for him as we wandered over the grassy hills and Pachamama standing guard over a fortress that connects to the in-betweens of time. Colibri started as the archetype of the Andean symbol of a messenger, but became more involved in the journey of our Time Migrant.

The original one- and two-liners came from a place of introspection and reflection of my family's history, indigeneity, and how that relates to the phenomena of migration and what it means to "find home" and "belong." Assimilation versus integration. I think of the insidiousness and violence of erasure. What if you were forced to leave home, what would you do to get back? Or what if your home is somewhere you haven't been yet, how far would you travel to find it? What if home is really in the hearts of those who hold you dearest?

Fortitude and hope are the undercurrent of Yupanki's story. He may not remember much and we may not be sure why or how he ended up as *un viajero*, but he has dreams to guide him.

I'm incredibly grateful to my partner B for her unwavering support, being a willing sounding board, and keeping me honest with myself throughout the writing and recording of the *Un Lugar Lejos* EP and chapbook. Especially for her patience with hearing the recordings happen. As one could imagine, writing and recording and listening to looper-based music can quickly get repetitive.

Thank you to those who read through sections of this book as it came together. And of course, thanks to the audio engineers that took on the musical element of *Un Lugar Lejos* - Storm Paul (*Un Lugar Lejos - EP, 2022*) and Anthony Defabritus/antFARM(studio) (*Vessels EP, 2023*). The music is half the experience, and I can't thank you enough for helping bring the recordings to fruition.

To those who have been to a Yupanki performance or a reading or may attend their first one in the future, thank you for being part of this shared experience.

I hope you enjoy the beginning of Yupanki's story. There is still much to discover and a long way to travel. I'm looking forward to seeing where it takes Yupanki and me. We'll see you somewhere along the way.

Gregg Yupanki Bautista
February 19, 2024

Gregg Yupanki Bautista is a musician, artist, and writer based in NJ. He lives in the Sourlands with his partner Breona and their dog Oates.

You can find him online at www.greggbautista.com.
His music can be found at www.yupankisounds.com.

Un Lugar Lejos - EP and *Vessels EP* are available on major streaming platforms.

www.ingramcontent.com/pod-product-compliance
Lightning Source LLC
Chambersburg PA
CBHW070600160726
48003CB00005B/2096